This book belongs to:

The Bright Idea :
The Story of Thomas Edison

Text © Ann Moore 1997

Illustrations © Mike Adams 1997

First published in Great Britain in 1997

by Macdonald Young Books

超級科學家系列
SUPER SCIENTISTS

電燈的發明：
愛迪生的故事

Ann Moore 著

Mike Adams 繪

洪瑞霞 譯

三民書局

The sound of magic

$\mathbb{M}$arion **tapped** on the **transmitter** over and over again. **Dot dash** dash dot — dot dash. Dot dash dash dot — dot dash. The **Morse Code** spelt the letters PA. Marion sighed **impatiently** as she waited for her Pa. He said he had a surprise and she wanted to see it.

"Oh Dot, do be quiet!" He suddenly **appeared** in the doorway.

神奇的聲音

　　瑪莉安在電報傳輸機上一遍又一遍地敲打著，發出了一陣陣嘟嘟吖吖的聲音。摩斯電碼解讀出字母PA。瑪莉安不耐煩地嘆著氣等她爸爸。他說有個令人驚喜的消息，她好想親眼瞧瞧。

　　突然，爸爸出現在門口叫著：「嘿！嘟嘟！安靜一點好不好！」

tap [tæp] 動 輕敲
transmitter [træns`mɪtɚ] 名 傳輸機
dot [dɑt] 名 點（摩斯電碼·）
dash [dæʃ] 名 線（摩斯電碼——）
Morse Code 摩斯電碼
　《美國人Samuel F. B. Morse
　　[1791–1872]所發明，由點和線
　　組成》
code [kod] 名 密碼
impatiently [ɪm`peʃəntlɪ] 副 不耐煩地
appear [ə`pɪr] 動 出現

Marion's father was the famous American scientist, Thomas Edison. Because he'd worked with Morse Code transmitters for many years, he'd **nicknamed** her Dot. Her brother Tom was Dash.

"Hurry up!" Marion **tugged** Edison's hand. "I want to see the surprise in the **laboratory**."

4

瑪莉安的爸爸是美國有名的科學家——湯瑪士·愛迪生。因為他多年來研究摩斯電碼傳輸機，便暱稱瑪莉安為嘟嘟，她的弟弟湯姆就叫做吁吁囉！

　　「快一點啦！」瑪莉安拉著愛迪生的手說：「我要去看實驗室裡的大驚喜。」

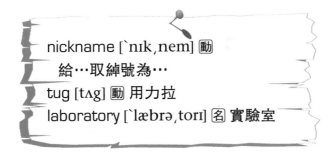

nickname [`nɪk,nem] 動
　給…取綽號為…
tug [tʌg] 動 用力拉
laboratory [`læbrə,torɪ] 名 實驗室

Marion ran along beside Pa as they crossed the grass to the long wooden laboratory. They hurried upstairs to join Edison's **assistants** round a **workbench**. Marion smiled excitedly at everyone.

6

瑪莉安在爸爸的旁邊跑著，穿過草坪，來到了木造的長型實驗室。他們急忙地上樓，和愛迪生的助理一起圍在工作檯旁。瑪莉安興奮地朝著每個人微笑。

assistant [ə`sɪstənt] 图 助手
workbench [`wɝk,bɛntʃ] 图 工作檯

"There!" Edison **swept** a cover off the end of the bench. Marion felt **disappointed**. Was this the surprise? All she could see was a **solid** metal tube wrapped in **tinfoil**, with a **handle** through it. A needle from a smaller tube at the side had made **marks** on the tinfoil.

愛迪生掀開桌角的蓋布嚷著：「看這邊喔！」瑪莉安有點兒失望，這算驚喜嗎？她看到的只是一根包著錫箔紙、硬梆梆的金屬管，旁邊還連著一個把手。從旁邊另一根較小的管子中，有根針可以在錫箔紙上留下一些記號。

sweep [swip] 動 清除，掃除
disappointed [,dɪsə`pɔɪntɪd] 形
　失望的
solid [`salɪd] 形 堅固的
tinfoil [`tɪn,fɔɪl] 名 錫箔
handle [`hændl̩] 名 把手
mark [mɑrk] 名 記號

"**R**eady?" Pa turned the handle.

Mary had a little lamb, its fleece was white as snow.

Marion heard Pa's voice. Then she watched him **sneeze**, but the **rhyme** didn't stop. How could Pa sneeze and yet go on speaking at the same time? He turned the handle faster and his voice went higher. It must be a **trick**!

「準備好了嗎？」爸爸搖搖機器的把手說。

瑪莉有隻羊咩咩，羊兒的毛白似雪。

瑪莉安聽到爸爸的聲音，然後她看到爸爸在打噴嚏，可是這韻詩並沒有停止。爸爸怎麼能一邊打噴嚏一邊還繼續說話呢？他把手搖得越快，聲音就變得越高。這裡面一定有什麼機關！

sneeze [sniz] 勔 打噴嚏
rhyme [raɪm] 名 韻詩
trick [trɪk] 名 戲法，魔術

Pa's **engineer**, Charles Batchelor, laughed at Marion's **puzzled expression**.

"It's a **phonograph**!" he **announced**. "Your father has **invented** an amazing machine which **records** sounds and then plays them back."

"What we say today, we could listen to again and again, Dot!"

爸爸的工程師查理・貝切勒看瑪莉安一臉狐疑，不禁笑了起來。

　　「這是留聲機呢！」他宣佈說：「妳爸爸發明了這臺令人驚奇的機器，可以用來收錄聲音，然後再播出來。」

　　「嘟嘟，我們今天所說的話，以後可以放出來聽好多次呢！」

engineer [ˌɛndʒəˈnɪr] 名 工程師
puzzled [ˈpʌzḷd] 形 困惑的
expression [ɪkˈsprɛʃən] 名 表情
phonograph [ˈfonəˌgræf] 名 留聲機
announce [əˈnaʊns] 動 宣佈
invent [ɪnˈvɛnt] 動 發明
record [rɪˈkɔrd] 動 記錄

Pa couldn't hide his **excitement**. "Think how useful that could be," he said as he **patted** the machine. "This baby's going to be very important!"

"Can I have a go?" asked Marion **shyly**.

For an hour Marion and her father played with the phonograph. She recorded a poem and everyone cheered when it was played back.

14

爸爸掩不住內心的狂喜，輕拍著機器說：「想想這發明有多大的用處！這寶貝將會變得很重要喲！」

　　「我可以試試看嗎？」瑪莉安害羞地問。

　　瑪莉安和爸爸玩留聲機玩了一小時，她錄了一首詩。當這首詩被播放出來時，大家都歡呼了起來。

excitement [ɪk`saɪtmənt] 名 興奮
pat [pæt] 動 輕拍
shyly [`ʃaɪlɪ] 副 害羞地

Then Edison **frowned** and **scratched** his head. "**Electricity**," he said **thoughtfully**. "I wonder if our phonograph could be worked by electricity?" He turned back to the bench, and Marion knew he'd forgotten all about her.

然後愛迪生皺了皺眉，抓了抓頭。「電！」他若有所思地說。「我在想，我們的留聲機可不可以用電來運轉？」他隨即轉身回工作檯。瑪莉安知道，爸爸此時根本就把她忘了。

frown [fraʊn] 動 皺眉
scratch [skrætʃ] 動 抓
electricity [ɪ,lɛk`trɪsətɪ] 名 電
thoughtfully [`θɔtfəlɪ] 副 沈思地

All about Pa

Late one night, Marion **crept** into the laboratory alone. A single gas lamp burned near the bench where her father sat, staring at a glass **globe**. **Dodging** past benches **cluttered** with **instruments** and books, she hurried over to him. "Pa!"

Startled, Edison dropped his pencil. It rolled into the shadows. "Dot! What are you doing here? You should be in bed." He looked **cross**.

18

有關爸爸的一切

　　有一天深夜，瑪莉安一個人溜進了爸爸的實驗室。工作檯附近點著一盞煤氣燈，愛迪生獨自坐在桌前，盯著一個玻璃燈泡看。她閃過亂七八糟堆滿儀器和書的工作檯，快步走過去，並叫了聲「爸！」

　　愛迪生嚇了一跳，手上的鉛筆也跟著掉到地上，滾進陰暗處去。「嘟嘟！妳在這裡做什麼？妳應該在床上睡覺才對啊！」他面帶怒色地說。

creep [krip] 動 躡足而行

globe [glob] 名 球，球狀物

dodge [dɑdʒ] 動 閃開

clutter [`klʌtɚ] 動 將…亂堆

instrument [`ɪnstrəmənt] 名 儀器

startle [`stɑrtl̩] 動 使…嚇了一跳

cross [krɔs] 形 不高興的

"**S**orry, Pa," Marion said quietly, "I know you're busy, but I've got something to show you. Look!" Marion pushed her school **report** into his hands. She watched closely as her father read the report.

"Well done!" he said at last. "You've done much better than I ever did at school."

"But you're really clever!" cried Marion in **amazement**.

「對不起啦！爸！」瑪莉安輕聲地說。「我知道你很忙，可是我有東西要給你。看！」瑪莉安把她的成績單放在愛迪生的手上。爸爸看著成績單，她一邊很仔細地觀察爸爸的神情。

　　「很好啊！」他看完後說。「你的表現比我當年在學校好得太多了！」

　　「可是你真的很聰明啊！」瑪莉安驚訝地說。

report [rɪ`port] 图 成績單
amazement [ə`mezmənt] 图 驚訝

"**H**mmm," sighed Pa. "I'm afraid my teachers didn't think so — they said I was too stupid, so your gran taught me at home. She even let me have a laboratory in our **cellar**. And that's when I started to invent things..."

"Did an **experiment** make you **deaf**?" Marion asked. She knew he didn't hear well.

「嗯！」愛迪生嘆了口氣說：「我的老師可不這麼認為。他們都說我實在太笨了。所以妳奶奶只好在家裡親自教我，她還幫我在地下室弄了個實驗室，我就是從那個時候開始發明東西的……」

　　「你的聽力不好是實驗的關係嗎？」瑪莉安問，她知道爸爸的耳朵不太好。

cellar [`sɛlɚ] 名 地下室
experiment [ɪk`spɛrəmənt] 名 實驗
deaf [dɛf] 形 聾的

"**N**o. I sold newspapers on the railroad when I was younger. Once, I nearly missed a train and someone pulled me **aboard** by my ears. I'm sure that made me deaf! That's why I **improved** Bell's telephone — so that I can hear it better. Now, isn't it time that you were in bed?"

"What's this?" Marion picked up the globe, pretending not to hear him.

"Careful!" Edison breathed a sigh of **relief** when it was safely in his hands. "It's my **glow bulb**, something I've been working on for years. And so has Joseph Swan in England. We want to **light** rooms using electricity **instead of** gas."

「不是的。我年輕時曾在火車上賣報紙。有一次，我差點趕不上車，有個人拉著我的耳朵把我拖上了車，我想那才是我耳朵不好的原因吧！也就是因為這樣，我才想去改良貝爾發明的電話，讓自己聽得清楚些。現在妳是不是應該回房睡覺了呢？」

「這是什麼？」瑪莉安假裝沒聽到，抓起了個玻璃球問。

「小心點！」愛迪生把球安全接過手來，這才鬆了口氣。「這是我研究多年的發亮燈泡，英格蘭有個叫喬瑟夫・史旺的人也在研究這玩意兒。我們希望可以用電——而不是煤氣——來照亮房間。」

aboard [ə`bord] 副 上車
improve [ɪm`pruv] 動 改良
relief [rɪ`lif] 名 放心
glow [glo] 名 白光；熾熱
bulb [bʌlb] 名 燈泡
light [laɪt] 動 照亮
instead of 代替

25

"How?" asked Marion. Sometimes her father had the strangest ideas.

"Well," he **explained**, "first we take all the air out of a bulb like this to make a **vacuum**. Then a **current** of electricity passes through a **filament** inside..."

「怎麼做呢？」瑪莉安問。爸爸時常會有一些奇奇怪怪的想法。

「這個嘛！」他解釋著。「首先我們把燈泡裡面的空氣抽光，就像這樣，在裡面造成一種真空狀態，然後再讓電流通過裝在裡面的蕊絲……」

explain [ɪk`splen] 動 解釋
vacuum [`vækjuəm] 名 真空
current [`kɜənt] 名 電流
filament [`fɪləmənt] 名 蕊絲

"What's a filament?"

"It's a thin length of metal or **carbon**. The electricity makes the filament so hot that it lights up. Trouble is, I don't know what to use to make a strong enough filament."

Marion thought for a minute. "**String**? That doesn't break."

「什麼是蕊絲啊！」

「就是一條金屬或碳做成的細絲。電流會把它變得很熱很熱，然後它就會發亮。問題是，我不知道怎樣才能做成一條夠堅韌的蕊絲。」

瑪莉安想了一會兒說：「用繩子呀！繩子是不會斷的。」

carbon [`karbən] 名 碳
string [strɪŋ] 名 繩子

Edison laughed. "No, that wouldn't work. It has to be very thin and able to **stand** very high **temperatures**." They both stared at the globe in silence, before Edison looked **pointedly** at the clock.

"All right, I'm going," said Marion **reluctantly** and went to bed.

愛迪生笑著說：「那是行不通的。我要的蕊絲要很細，而且得耐得住高溫。」他們倆靜靜地望著那個燈泡一會兒，愛迪生暗示性地用眼睛看了看時鐘。

「好啦！我回去睡覺啦！」瑪莉安心不甘情不願地說著，然後走回了臥房。

stand [stænd] 動 承受，忍耐
temperature [`tɛmprətʃɚ] 名 溫度
pointdely [`pɔɪntɪdlɪ] 副 有所指地
reluctantly [rɪ`lʌktəntlɪ] 副 不情願地

There must be a way

While Marion slept, her father returned to his problem.

"The filament," he **muttered**. He tugged his right **eyebrow**, something he often did when he was thinking. "I've tried burning strips of paper, wood, corn **stalks** to make carbon filaments, but none of them work. There must be a way — there must be something we haven't thought of." He tugged his eyebrow again.

一定有辦法

　　瑪莉安回去睡覺後，愛迪生又回到了他的問題上。

　　「這蕊絲……」愛迪生喃喃地唸著。他揚了揚右邊的眉毛，這是他思考時常做的動作。「我已經試過用燃燒的紙條、木條及玉蜀黍梗製成的碳質蕊絲，但沒有一樣成功。一定有辦法可以行得通，只是我們還沒想到而已。」他又揚了揚眉毛。

mutter [ˋmʌtɚ] 動 嘀咕，喃喃低語
eyebrow [ˋaɪ͵braʊ] 名 眉毛
stalk [stɔk] 名 梗；莖

He was still there at eight o'clock the next morning when Charles Batchelor arrived. Charles, a British engineer, was Edison's **right-hand man** at the laboratory. "Good morning!" he said, then stopped and stared.

On the bench a large light bulb was glowing **faintly**.

清晨八點，<u>查理‧貝切勒</u>來到實驗室時，愛迪生仍待在那裡。這位英國的工程師查理，是愛迪生在實驗室裡的得力助手。「早安！」他說，然後便停下來盯著眼前的景象。

　　在工作檯上，一個大燈泡正發出微弱的亮光。

right-hand [`raɪt`hænd] 形 可依靠的
right-hand man　得力助手
faintly [`fentlɪ] 副 微弱地

"**I**'ve done it!" shouted Edison. "An **electric** light bulb with a filament of thin **platinum**! The light isn't **steady**, but it **lasts** longer than anything else we've tried. We'll have to make it stronger, of course."

"**Congratulations**!" Batchelor **grinned** and shook his hand **vigorously**.

「我成功了！」愛迪生喊叫起來。「這是一個細鉑蕊心的電燈泡。它發出的亮光雖然不穩定，但卻比我們以前試過的任何材質都要持久些。當然，我們還要讓它再耐久一點。」

「恭喜囉！」貝切勒咧嘴笑著，用力地握住愛迪生的手。

electric [ɪ`lɛktrɪk] 形 電的
platinum [`plætṇəm] 名 鉑
steady [`stɛdɪ] 形 穩定的
last [læst] 動 持續
congratulation [kən͵grætʃə`leʃən] 感 恭喜
　（通常congratulations）
grin [grɪn] 動 咧嘴笑
vigorously [`vɪgərəslɪ] 副 強而有力地

"And we must improve the globe too." Edison **paced** the floor. "The size will **affect** the light, and the vacuum must be as good as possible. Any air inside and the filament burns out too quickly."

"But what about Joseph Swan?" Batchelor **interrupted**. Joseph Swan, the British **physicist**, had been trying to make an electric light bulb for years.

「燈泡本身也應該改良一下。」愛迪生在房裡來回踱步地說：「燈泡的大小會影響亮度，裡面也要盡可能抽成真空。只要有一點空氣，燈絲一下子就會燒掉。」

「喬瑟夫・史旺那裡進展如何呢？」貝切勒打斷愛迪生問。那位英國的物理學家已經研究電燈泡很多年了。

pace [pes] 動 在（某處）踱步
affect [ə`fɛkt] 動 影響
interrupt [,ɪntə`rʌpt] 動 打斷
physicist [`fɪzəsɪst] 名 物理學家

Edison stopped pacing. "As far as I know," he said, "he hasn't made a successful light bulb — yet."

"Then you must **apply** for a **patent** right away!" exclaimed Batchelor. "Then no one else can steal your idea."

A few months later, Batchelor burst into the laboratory waving a newspaper. "Look," he said. "It says that Swan has **demonstrated** a light bulb in England. His filament was made of silk thread, but it only glowed for a few minutes. Do you think we'll be the first to make the perfect light bulb now?"

愛迪生停止了踱步說：「就我所知，他還沒有成功做出燈泡來。」

「那你應該趕緊去申請專利呀！」貝切勒聽了大聲說著：「這樣別人才不能抄襲你的想法。」

幾個月後，貝切勒揮動著手上的報紙衝進實驗室。「看！」他說。「報紙上說史旺已經在英格蘭展示他發明的燈泡，燈泡的蕊心是用細絲線做成的，不過它只亮了幾分鐘而已。你想，我們會不會成為第一個做出完美燈泡的人呢？」

apply [ə`plaɪ] 動 申請
patent [`pætn̩t] 名 專利
demonstrate [`dɛmən‚stret] 動 展示

41

The race is on

"**P**a, are you coming on the picnic?" It was the Sunday after 4 July and Marion was hoping that he'd spend the day with them again. They'd had a **terrific** time on **Independence Day** with **firecrackers** and paper hats. After dinner Pa had played the organ and everyone had sung.

Now, however, Pa shook his head.

競爭持續進行

　　「爸！你要一起來野餐嗎？」這是七月四日國慶日後的
禮拜天，瑪莉安希望爸爸可以再陪他們一天。國慶日那天，
他們戴著紙帽、放著煙火，玩得開心極了。晚餐後，爸爸還
彈了風琴，大家一起唱歌。

　　可是爸爸卻搖了搖頭。

terrific [tə`rɪfɪk] 形 極佳的
independence [ˌɪndɪ`pɛndəns] 名 獨立
Independence Day　美國獨立紀念日，
　美國國慶（七月四日）
firecracker [`faɪrˌkrækɚ] 名 煙火

"Sorry, Dot, not today — I've got far too much work to do. I must **solve** some problems with the glow bulb. It will only burn for a few minutes, but I want to be the first to make it burn for hours, even months," he said thoughtfully. "I know all the ways that don't work, but not the one that does!" And with that, he **wandered** out of the room.

「很抱歉，嘟嘟，今天實在不行，我有太多工作要做了！我一定得把燈泡的問題解決。它現在只能亮幾分鐘而已，而我希望我是第一個能使它亮個幾小時、甚至幾個月的人。」他若有所思地說。「現在我知道哪些方法是行不通的，但卻不知道哪個方法才行得通！」說著說著，他慢慢走出了房間。

solve [sɑlv] 動 解決
wander [`wɑndɚ] 動 恍惚；出神

All summer, Pa worked on his electric light bulb. He and his assistants tried to improve the bulb's shape and vacuum. They tried to find the best shape for the filament. And they tried to make it stronger.

"We've also got to find a way of **dividing** the **electric current** between the lamps," Edison told his assistants. "At the moment, if one goes out, they all go out. That's no use! If we're going to invent something, it's got to be useful to everyone and something everyone can **afford**."

整個夏天，爸爸都在研究他的電燈泡。他和他的助理們想盡辦法去改良燈泡的形狀和裡面的真空狀態。他們也試著找出蕊絲的最佳形狀，也想讓它再強韌些。

　　「我們還要想辦法使電流分散到各盞燈去。」愛迪生告訴他的助手。「現在的情形是，如果一盞燈熄了，其他的就跟著熄掉，這樣沒什麼用！如果我們要發明一樣東西，就必須要好用，而且是要大家都負擔得起的。」

divide [də`vaɪd] 動 分開
electric current　電流
afford [ə`ford] 動 負擔得起

One evening, Marion and her mother took Pa his supper. They found him asleep with his head on the workbench. "We won't wake him," Ma **whispered** as they left quietly. "He'll just go on working when he wakes. That's the way he is." And she smiled.

有天晚上，瑪莉安和媽媽幫爸爸端來了晚餐，卻發現爸爸趴在工作檯上睡著了。「別叫醒他！」媽媽輕聲地說，帶著她悄悄地離開。「他一醒來就會繼續工作的，這就是妳爸爸啊！」瑪莉安會心地笑了。

whisper [ˋhwɪspɚ] 動 輕聲地說

Little globes of sunshine

One October morning, a year after he had **patented** his light bulb, Edison burst into the kitchen. "I want a large **bobbin** of cotton," he **demanded**.

"What's it for?" Marion asked as he took the bobbin.

"Just an experiment," her father answered. He turned abruptly and was gone.

Marion felt cross. Why was she never allowed to help?

發出太陽光的小球

在愛迪生申請燈泡專利一年後，某個十月的早晨，愛迪生衝進廚房嚷著：「給我一大球棉線。」

「做什麼用啊？」瑪莉安問著拿了棉球的爸爸。

「只是做實驗啦！」爸爸回答，然後很快便轉身不見。

瑪莉安有點生氣，為什麼爸爸從來不讓她幫忙呢？

patent [`pætn̩t] 動 獲得…的專利
bobbin [`bɑbɪn] 名 線軸
demand [dɪ`mænd] 動 要求

51

Across in the laboratory, Edison said to Batchelor, "Right. Platinum won't do. It's not bright enough. Swan used silk thread, we'll try cotton."

For two days and nights Edison and Batchelor tried to make a filament by **baking** lengths of cotton into carbon threads. Time and time again the threads broke, but still they went on trying. On the morning of the third day, Batchelor whispered at last, "I've done it. Let's put it in the globe." Very carefully, he and Edison carried the filament to the globe — and it broke.

"**O**h dear," Edison **groaned**. "Thinking of an idea is easy. It's making it work that's hard!"

After many more hours they had made another filament, but it broke again. Evening came, but they worked on.

到了實驗室，愛迪生告訴貝切勒：「我知道了，鉑絲是不行的，它還不夠亮。史旺用細絲線，那我們就試試棉線吧！」

　　接下來的兩天兩夜，愛迪生和貝切勒試著把棉線烘成他們要的碳絲。碳絲斷了一次又一次，但他們還是繼續嘗試。到了第三天早上，貝切勒終於輕聲地說：「我成功了！我們把它放進燈泡內試試看。」他和愛迪生小心翼翼地把完成的碳絲拿到燈泡旁邊——但它還是斷掉了。

bake [bek] 動 烘

「唉呀！」愛迪生發著牢騷。「想得容易，做起來可真難囉！」

　　又經過好幾個小時，他們做出了另一條蕊絲，可惜又斷了。天黑了，但他們仍繼續努力著。

groan [gron] 動 發牢騷

After tea on that third day Marion decided that she must see what Pa was doing. She crept silently into the laboratory. Pa and Batchelor bent over their glow bulb. Marion **tiptoed** nearer and hid beneath a bench.

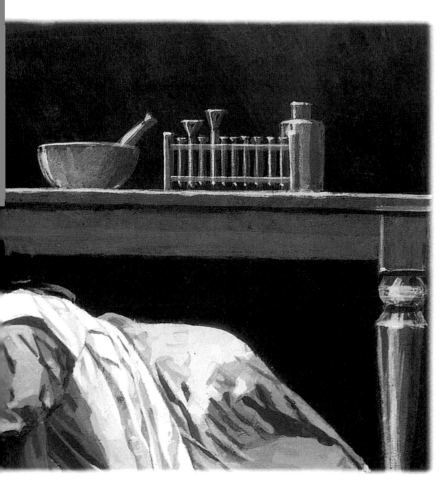

Her father carefully **balanced** a fine thread in the globe. Batchelor **pumped** out all the air and **sealed** the bulb.

"Third time lucky," she heard Pa say. "**Switch** it **on**."

到了第三天，喝過午茶後，瑪莉安決定去看看爸爸到底在做什麼。她悄悄地溜進實驗室，爸爸和貝切勒正全心全意地研究著他們的燈泡。瑪莉安躡手躡腳地再靠近一些，躲在一張桌子底下。

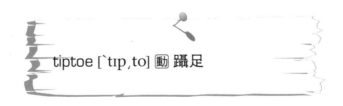

tiptoe [`tɪp,to] 勔 躡足

她爸爸小心翼翼地維持細絲在燈泡裡的平衡，貝切勒則把空氣全部抽出，並且封住燈泡。

　　「第三次了，祝我們好運！」她聽見爸爸說。「打開電源。」

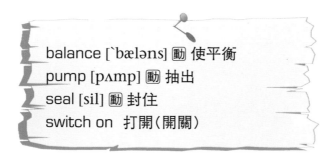

balance [ˋbæləns] 勔 使平衡
pump [pʌmp] 勔 抽出
seal [sil] 勔 封住
switch on 打開（開關）

A pale light glowed. "More current." The current was **increased** and still the bulb burned **steadily**. Marion jumped out of her hiding place.

"Hooray!" she shouted, and her father was so pleased with his experiment that he forgot to be cross with her for **sneaking** in. The bulb glowed for hours before it **burned out**. And the next bulb burned for even longer!

一抹微弱的光亮了起來。「加強電流量。」電力加強了，燈泡仍穩定地發出亮光。瑪莉安從藏身之處跳了出來。

「哇塞！」她興奮地叫著。愛迪生太高興了，竟忘了要責備瑪莉安為什麼偷溜了進來。這個燈泡就這樣亮了好幾個小時，下一個燈泡甚至亮了更久。

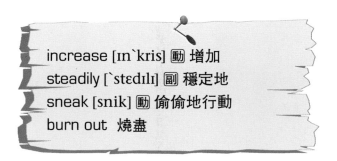

increase [ɪnˋkris] 勔 增加
steadily [ˋstɛdɪlɪ] 副 穩定地
sneak [snik] 勔 偷偷地行動
burn out 燒盡

"**I**f it can burn for forty hours, I can make it last a hundred!" Edison exclaimed.

"Ma, look how many people there are!" Marion stood at the window. A steady stream of visitors walked past on their way to the laboratory. So many people had asked to see Edison's new light bulb, that he'd opened his **workshop** to the **public**.

「如果它可以亮四十個小時，我就有辦法讓它持續到一百個小時！」愛迪生大聲地喊著。

　　瑪莉安站在窗戶旁叫道：「媽！快來看！好多人在外面喔！」群眾陸陸續續來到愛迪生的實驗室。好多人央求一睹愛迪生的新燈泡，他只好把實驗室開放給民眾參觀。

workshop [`wɝk͵ʃɑp] 图 工作室
public [`pʌblɪk] 图 群眾

Inside, Edison spoke to newspaper **reporters**, while machines made light bulbs faster than any human could.

"Gee," said one reporter. "These bulbs are like little globes of sunshine."

"Yes sir," agreed an old man nearby. He **peered** at the bulb. "But I can't work out how you get that red-hot **wire** in there."

Edison and Batchelor, remembering what a struggle they'd had, smiled at each other.

在實驗室裡，愛迪生接受記者訪問的同時，機器也以人力所不及的速度製造著燈泡。

　　「哦唷！」其中一位記者說：「這些燈泡就像一顆顆小太陽。」

　　「是呀！」旁邊一個長者同意地附和。他直盯著燈泡瞧呀瞧的。「不過我就是想不透，你們是如何把那熾熱的紅鐵絲放在裡面的？」

　　愛迪生和貝切勒想起他們奮鬥的歷程，不禁相視而笑。

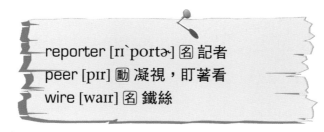

reporter [rɪˋportɚ] 名 記者
peer [pɪr] 動 凝視，盯著看
wire [waɪr] 名 鐵絲

The 'universal lamplighter'

For a while, Edison continued to work on his electric light. But as usual, he was busy with other ideas as well.

"Wheee!" Marion and Tom **clung** together as Pa's latest invention **bumped** along a newly laid track beside the workshops. They were **squashed** beside Pa, as he drove a small electric train round the **grounds**.

照亮世界的人

　　有好一陣子，愛迪生仍繼續研究他的電燈，但和往常一樣，他還有許許多多的想法，夠他忙的呢！

　　「哇！哇！……」當爸爸的最新發明在實驗室旁新鋪的軌道上顛簸前進時，瑪莉安和湯姆緊緊地抱在一起。他們擠坐在爸爸旁邊，而爸爸則開著一輛小電車在兜圈子。

cling [klɪŋ] 動 抓住，摟住（過去式clung [klʌŋ]）
bump [bʌmp] 動 顛簸行進
squash [skwɑʃ] 動 擠壓
ground [graund] 名 地面

"**H**old on tight," he shouted. "We're traveling at 25 miles an hour — and I can make it go faster!" Behind him, a group of laboratory workers and newspaper reporters **jolted** about in an open wooden carriage. Then the train stopped. "Nearly three-quarters of a mile!" Pa **beamed** at everyone. "Electricity! There are so many ways it will help us if we use it properly."

Two years later Edison's electric lights had been **exhibited** in France and England, and even used on a ship.

"Today is the greatest **adventure** of my life," he said to Marion. "Today, 4 September 1882, I open the first **commercial** electric power station in America. It will light bulbs in more than two hundred buildings here in Pearl Street, New York."

「抓緊了！」愛迪生喊著。「我們接著要以時速二十五英里的速度前進——還可以跑得更快喔！」一群實驗室工作人員及記者坐在爸爸身後的木製車廂裡，隨著電車的顛簸不時地晃動著。電車終於停了下來。「我們大概走了四分之三英里喲！」爸爸容光煥發地對著每個人微笑。「這就是電啊！如果我們好好利用它，它可以幫我們不少忙呢！」

jolt [dʒolt] 動 顛簸，搖晃
beam [bim] 動 開朗地微笑

兩年後，愛迪生發明的電燈在法國及英格蘭展出，這個發明甚至被應用在船艦上。

　　「今天是我這一生中最棒的時刻。」愛迪生告訴瑪莉安。「今天，西元一八八二年九月四日，我啟用了美國第一個商用發電所。這個發電所可以使紐約珍珠街上兩百多棟建築物的燈泡同時亮起來。」

exhibit [ɪgˋzɪbɪt] 動 展示
adventure [ədˋvɛntʃɚ] 名 冒險
commercial [kəˋmɝʃəl] 形 商業性的

At three o'clock that afternoon the **generators hummed**. Would they make enough electricity? Everyone held their breath. Then bulbs glowed and everyone cheered. The electric light **age** had really begun.

Soon, electric power was being supplied to homes, hotels, theaters and mills.

"Look Pa, you're famous."

Proudly, Marion held out the *New York Times*. "They're calling you the **universal** lamplighter!"

下午三點鐘，發電機正式啟動。電力夠不夠呢？大家都屏息以待。果然，街上的燈一個個亮了起來，大家熱情地歡呼，電燈的時代終於來臨了。

很快地，一般的家庭、旅館、戲院及磨坊都有了電力的供給。

「爸！你看！你出名了！」

瑪莉安驕傲地指著《紐約時報》說。「他們說你是照亮世界的人呢！」

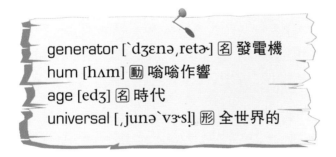

generator [ˈdʒɛnəˌretə] 图 發電機
hum [hʌm] 動 嗡嗡作響
age [edʒ] 图 時代
universal [ˌjunəˈvɝsl] 形 全世界的

Edison died in 1931. After his funeral, Marion watched as all the lights of America **dimmed** for a minute in memory of her father. Even the **Statue of Liberty's torch** went out. Then electricity hummed again and lights **blazed** everywhere. America and the world knew just how much they **owed** to Thomas Edison and his study of electricity.

74

愛迪生於西元一九三一年逝世。在他的葬禮後，瑪莉安凝望著全美熄燈一分鐘以追悼她的父親，甚至自由女神手上的火炬也不例外。接著電力恢復，所有的燈又歸於絢爛。美國和全世界的人都知道，這一切都要歸功於愛迪生以及他在電力上的發明研究。

dim [dɪm] 勔 變暗
statue [`stætʃʊ] 图 雕像
Statue of Liberty　自由女神像
torch [tɔrtʃ] 图 火炬
blaze [blez] 勔 閃耀
owe [o] 勔 歸功

Timeline

Thomas Edison was born on 11 February 1847 in Milan, Ohio, USA.

1855 *Edison leaves school after three months.*

1863 *Becomes an apprentice telegrapher, work he continues until 1868.*

1871 *Develops Scholes' typewriter. Marries Mary Stilwell.*

1872 *Daughter Marion is born.*

1876 *Builds his laboratory at Menlo Park, New Jersey. Son Thomas is born.*

1877 *Improves the telephone. Tests the phonograph.*

1879 *Patents the light bulb.*

1880 *Joseph Swan patents his light bulb. Edison carries out the electric railway experiment at Menlo Park.*

1882	Pearl Street Generating Station is switched on.
1891	Patents the kinetoscope.
1899	Begins work on electric car batteries.
1912	Works with Henry Ford to invent a self-starter for Ford's cars.
1914– 1918	Works with the US Navy to develop torpedo detection.
1927	Sets up a laboratory in Florida to research rubber.
1928	Awarded a Gold Medal by Congress for his work and inventions.

Thomas Edison died on 18 October 1931 in New Jersey, USA. He was 84 years old.

生平紀事

一八四七年二月十一日，湯瑪士・愛迪生出生於美國俄亥俄州米蘭市。

1855　愛迪生上學三個月後便輟學。

1863　擔任電報發送見習生，一直做到一八六八年。

1871　改良史庫爾的打字機。與瑪莉・史帝威爾結婚。

1872　女兒瑪莉安出生。

1876　在紐澤西州門羅公園建造實驗室。兒子湯瑪士出生。

1877　改良電話。測試留聲機。

1879　申請燈泡專利。

1880　喬瑟夫・史旺申請燈泡專利。愛迪生在門羅公園進行有軌電車試驗。

1882　珍珠街發電所啟用。

1891　申請真空映像管專利。

1899　開始研究電車電池。

1912　與亨利・福特一起研發福特汽車自動起動裝置。

1914- 與美國海軍合作研發魚雷偵測器。

1918

1927　在佛羅里達州成立實驗室研究橡膠。

1928　美國國會頒贈黃金勳章表彰他的研究與發明。

一九三一年十月十八日，湯瑪士・愛迪生逝世於美國紐澤西州，享年八十四歲。

Glossary

current [ˋkɝənt] 名 電流
a flow of electricity

electricity [ɪ͵lɛkˋtrɪsətɪ] 名 電
a form of energy which uses tiny particles called electrons

filament [ˋfɪləmənt] 名 蕊絲
a thin metal wire, or coil of wire, which glows red or even
white-hot when electric current flows through it

generator [ˋdʒɛnə͵retɚ] 名 發電機
a machine used for changing movement into electricity

kinetoscope [kɪˋnitə͵skop] 名 電影放映機
the first machine to show moving pictures. It moved images
on strips of film so fast that figures on them seemed to move.

laboratory [ˋlæbrə͵torɪ] 名 實驗室
a building or room used for scientific experiments and
research

patent [ˋpætṇt] 名 專利
a document giving someone the sole right to make or sell an
invention

phonograph [ˋfonə͵græf] 名 留聲機
a machine for recording and playing back sounds. Edison first
used a tube, but later sound was recorded on flat discs.

transmitter [træns`mɪtɚ] 名 傳輸機

a piece of equipment or a machine which sends out signals or messages

vacuum [`vækjʊəm] 名 真空

a space from which all or most of the air has been removed

國家圖書館出版品預行編目資料

電燈的發明:愛迪生的故事=The bright idea:the story
of Thomas Edison / Ann Moore著;Mike Adams繪;
洪瑞霞譯.－－初版二刷.－－臺北市:三民, 2005
　　面;　　　公分.－－(超級科學家系列)
　ISBN 957－14－3016－1　(平裝)

　1.英國語言—讀本

805.18　　　　　　　　　　　　　　　　88004066

網路書店位址　http://www.sanmin.com.tw

© 　電燈的發明:愛迪生的故事

　著作人　Ann Moore
　繪圖者　Mike Adams
　譯　者　洪瑞霞
　發行人　劉振強
　發行所　三民書局股份有限公司
　　　　　地址／臺北市復興北路386號
　　　　　電話／(02)25006600
　　　　　郵撥／0009998-5
　印刷所　三民書局股份有限公司
　門市部　復北店／臺北市復興北路386號
　　　　　重南店／臺北市重慶南路一段61號
　初版一刷　1999年8月
　初版二刷　2005年7月
　編　號　S 854880
　定　價　新臺幣壹佰陸拾元整
　行政院新聞局登記證局版臺業字第○二○○號